The Butterfly in Me

By Trinette Davis

Illustrated by S. Cooper

Outskirts Press, Inc.
http://www.outskirtspress.com

ISBN: 978-1-4787-7930-8

Outskirts Press and the "OP" logo are trademarks belonging to Outskirts Press, Inc.

PRINTED IN THE UNITED STATES OF AMERICA

Dedicated to: _____

Dedication

"The Butterfly in Me" is the second book written out of a series titled Pucca's Great Discoveries. This book is about the feelings and emotions that a child goes through when they lose someone special to them. It is a wonderful story about how a big beautiful butterfly helps Pucca to finds some peace, courage and healing.

This book is also dedicated to all children that have been through this experience. I hope it will help them to find peace, courage, and healing.

One morning Pucca woke up feeling very sad and blue. She could not stop thinking about her favorite cousin and all the fun things they used to do.

Pucca could not understand why
her cousin had to get sick and go away.
They were like two peas in a pod
that were together almost every day.

This made Pucca feel very lonely and confused because every night she would dream about her cousin and she didn't know what to do.

Pucca thought she would never get
to see her cousin again in life.
She thought if she said a little prayer
then everything would be all right.

Until one bright sunny morning,
Pucca woke up and to her surprise
at her window there was
a big beautiful butterfly.

Pucca jumped out of the bed and ran
to the window to open it.
The big beautiful butterfly flew in
and then started to fly
all around her room whipping its wings
all over Pucca things.

Pucca was very excited and she started
singing and dancing all around her room.
She was chasing and playing
with the big beautiful butterfly
as if she had created her own tune.

The big beautiful butterfly would stay
for a while and then it would
soon fly out the window.
This made Pucca very happy
as she soon forgot about being
very sad, blue, lonely and confused.

This became a morning routine.
Whenever Pucca started feeling sad
or blue and lonely or confused
the big beautiful butterfly would appear
and magically make those feelings
disappear.

Pucca had come to realize
that the big beautiful butterfly
had become her friend.
It made her feel very special
and happy within.

Pucca then started to think about
her favorite cousin in a fun loving way.
She remembered just how much
her cousin loved butterflies
and that it was one of her
favorite things in the world.
Pucca smiled and then said yay.

Pucca thought about all this
for a few minutes.
She started to put it all together
but wait she wasn't finished.

She then realized that the
big beautiful butterfly only appeared
when she was feeling
sad, blue, lonely and confused.
She joyfully shouted out,
Tarae is that you!

The big beautiful butterfly then appeared,
fluttering its wings as it said
"yes, I never left you and
I will always be here within you".

The End

CPSIA information can be obtained at www.ICGtesting.com
Printed in the USA
BVIW12n1826221216
471650BV00008B/31